WORKING THE TWELVE STEPS

Keep It Simple Series

First published October, 1988.

Copyright © 1988, Hazelden Foundation.
All rights reserved. No portion of this publication
may be reproduced in any manner without the written
permission of the publisher.

ISBN: 0-89486-563-3

Printed in the United States of America.

Editor's Note:

Hazelden Educational Materials offers a variety of information on chemical dependency and related areas. Our publications do not necessarily represent Hazelden or its programs, nor do they officially speak for any Twelve Step organization.

CONTENTS

INTRODUCTION

Chemical dependency (an addiction to alcohol and other drugs) has been a problem for people for many years — maybe since humans learned that smoking or eating certain plants, or drinking aged fruit juice could make them feel good.

All through history we find warnings that too much liquor, or too much "locoweed," or too much tonic (old-time medicine) could make people become crazy. Many, many people died from that "craziness" that we now know is chemical dependency.

Until 1935, there was no known treatment that worked to help alcoholics and other drug addicts stop using mood-altering chemicals. That year the first real help for this problem was developed by alcoholics themselves. Two men, Bill W. and Dr. Bob, started a group called Alcoholics Anonymous. They met to help each other stay sober. They tried to become better people and fix up their lives. It worked. Finally there was a way for alcoholics to return to healthy living.

In 1939 the members of this group wrote a book called *Alcoholics Anonymous.* In this book they wrote about the Steps they took to recover from their disease. They suggested that other alcoholics could recover by taking these Steps.

The Twelve Steps of Alcoholics Anonymous

1. We admitted we were powerless over alcohol — that our lives had become unmanageable.
2. Came to believe that a Power greater than ourselves could restore us to sanity.
3. Made a decision to turn our will and our lives over to the care of God *as we understood Him.*
4. Made a searching and fearless moral inventory of ourselves.
5. Admitted to God, to ourselves, and to another human being the exact nature of our wrongs.
6. Were entirely ready to have God remove all these defects of character.
7. Humbly asked Him to remove our shortcomings.

8. Made a list of all persons we had harmed, and became willing to make amends to them all.

9. Made direct amends to such people wherever possible, except when to do so would injure them or others.

10. Continued to take personal inventory and when we were wrong promptly admitted it.

11. Sought through prayer and meditation to improve our conscious contact with God *as we understood Him,* praying only for knowledge of His will for us and the power to carry that out.

12. Having had a spiritual awakening as the result of these steps, we tried to carry this message to alcoholics, and to practice these principles in all our affairs.[*]

WHAT THE TWELVE STEPS TEACH US

These Twelve Steps are now used by people with all kinds of addictions and also by family members and friends who love them. No longer just for alcoholics, the Steps are the basis for many other recovery programs such as Al-Anon, Narcotics Anonymous, Gamblers Anonymous, and Overeaters Anonymous.

Principles Are Truths

The Steps are what the program refers to as "principles." A way to think about principles is that they are basic truths. Twelve Step programs are based on the truth that addicted people can recover from addiction by following these suggested Steps.

The Steps are designed to get and keep us sober. They are also designed to free us of our shame, worry, false pride, stubbornness, and fears.

Truths Require Rules

The Steps are "suggested." We alcohol and other drug addicts don't take suggestions very well. But if we want to become sober, we will need help. We truly don't know how to live sober. We've bounced through life going from one high to another, acting like we

[*] The Twelve Steps are taken from *Alcoholics Anonymous* (Third Edition), published by A.A. World Services, Inc., New York, N.Y., pp. 59-60. Reprinted with permission.

2

were in control. The Twelve Steps offer us a new way of life. They give us some basic rules for how to act.

Many of us thought we didn't need rules about how to act. We would act the way we wanted. We didn't care what anyone thought. The truth is that even in our addiction we had rules for how to act, but they were *addict's* rules.

Principles Become Beliefs

Principles are also beliefs. In recovery, the Twelve Steps will become beliefs for us. In this way the Steps become a *way of life.*

- We will come to see how our lives were unmanageable.
- We will come to believe we are powerless over alcohol and other drugs.
- We will come to believe that it is best for us to admit to others when we are wrong.
- We will come to believe serving and helping others is important.

These are just a few examples of the beliefs the Twelve Steps hold within them. The Twelve Steps hold all the beliefs and ideas we need to stay sober and to live spiritual and sane lives.

Giving Our Lives Order

Through the Twelve Steps we also find a way to put order into our lives.

We find a way to join our minds, bodies, emotions, and spirits.

We need this type of help because our illness taught us to be messy.

Addiction separates us from ourselves, our family and friends, and our Higher Power. We become lost. The Twelve Steps bring us back to ourselves, our family and friends, and our Higher Power. They do this by putting order back into our lives.

It takes a certain amount of work to live by the Twelve Steps. This is part of healing. In the past, we may have done whatever we wanted, whenever we wanted, not caring who suffered. We were self-centered. The Twelve Steps will help us become self- *and* other-centered.

They will teach us to think about our actions before we act. If actions might harm someone else, then we will not act that way no matter how much we want to.

Taking Responsibility

Our alcohol and other drug dependence taught us not to take responsibility for our actions. When we're working the Steps, we are honest about our actions. If something went wrong in the past, we would blame someone or something for the way we acted. The Twelve Steps teach us to be honest with ourselves, with others, and with our Higher Power.

The Twelve Steps teach us how to get back what we've lost to our addiction. In fact, over time we can get back all we've lost and more. By taking responsibility for ourselves, we stop the denial process that was the fuel for our addiction. Through the Twelve Steps, we learn that by taking responsibility for our actions we gain personal power.

We were experts at blaming others for our problems. The Twelve Steps teach us to look at ourselves and see how we created many of our problems. As we take responsibility for our actions we like ourselves better. In time, we begin to reach out to the world around us. We look to ourselves for answers instead of looking to drugs for answers. What a welcome relief!

Learning Self-Respect

The Twelve Steps teach us about ourselves. We learn and understand who we are and how we act.

The Steps teach us how to share our real selves with others and our Higher Power. We realize we are spiritual people, and we learn how to grow spiritually.

The Twelve Steps are a way for us to learn to care for ourselves and others again. The Steps are clear statements telling us what we need to do to make our lives easier. We choose to work them or not. They are a way for us to get self-respect back.

In working the Steps, life becomes a series of small ''wins'' for us. Thus, self-confidence returns and the world becomes less scary to us.

We learn how to care for and love ourselves in a lasting way. We are good people; we feel and believe this. So, in a very simple way, the Twelve Steps are about love — true self-love. We can't love others in a lasting way until we learn to love ourselves. The Twelve Steps give us the chance to love ourselves again.

STEP ONE

We admitted we were powerless over alcohol — that our lives had become unmanageable.

The First Step is our beginning. Like all firsts, it is very important. We can't make any gains in the other Steps until we grab hold of the First Step. Why? Because the First Step is the only Step that speaks directly to our dependence on alcohol and other drugs.

In taking the First Step we see and talk about the core part of our illness: the crazy relationship we had with alcohol and other drugs. The First Step gets us sober. The other eleven Steps will help us develop a way of life that will keep us sober.

Ours is an illness of body, mind, and spirit. The First Step is the only Step that asks us to remember and admit how our bodies got sick from using alcohol and other drugs. It reminds us how we are different from social users. We react differently when we take mood-changing chemicals. Our bodies become out of control. Signs of this are our increased tolerance, blackouts, cravings, and hangovers.

Sobriety means honesty. In Step One we are first faced with having to be honest. We learn this by admitting our loss of control. We have been out of control for a long time, but our denial has kept us from admitting the truth. Honesty will get us well.

If we truly work the First Step, we will feel a sense of relief. The First Step lets us out of our prison. Honesty will bring us happiness just as dishonesty made us sad and lonely. We can gain a great sense of peace from finally talking about what our illness has put us through. It has been said that in the First Step we find ourselves. This also means that if we ever feel lost in our program, we will find ourselves again if we look to the First Step for help.

Let's look at the main parts found in the First Step.

"We . . ."

The "we" of the First Step is very important to understand. Our illness caused us to be self-centered. As the Big Book says, we had become "self-will run riot." The only relationship that mattered was the one we had with our chemicals. We didn't care about anyone else. And if we are totally honest, we didn't even care for ourselves. We became loners. Those we hung around with were often as sick or sicker than we were. We didn't feel like we fit anywhere. The only folks who would have much to do with us were our drinking or using friends and maybe our families. And most of them were very tired of our childish ways.

The "we" of the First Step tells us we are now part of a loving community. We are with people like us. We are with people who understand. Because we have people to help us, we don't have to struggle alone anymore.

Ours is an illness that has to do with relationships. Our main relationship was with alcohol and other drugs. We trusted drugs more than we trusted people. We trusted drugs more than we trusted ourselves. We trusted drugs more than we trusted a Higher Power. We tried to get our emotional needs met through alcohol and other drugs, and not through people or a Higher Power. We came to believe that a relationship with alcohol and other drugs could truly make us happy. This was a sick relationship.

The "we" of the First Step is also about relationships. By working the First Step, we start to add honesty to our relationships. To work the First Step we need to believe we are one of many who suffer from this illness. We can't fight our illness alone. We tried and we got sicker. Other addicts can't fight their addiction alone: we need them and they need us. Because of this, the "we" of the program is formed, and we help to heal each other. It is as if each one of us holds a part of a puzzle and together we create the whole. In our relationship with alcohol and other drugs, we found sickness. In our relationships with other recovering addicts, we will find wellness.

". . . admitted . . ."

Admitting means honesty. The First Step is about getting honest. We had become slaves to our addiction — no ifs, ands, or buts about it. We had lost control.

A large part of our illness is *denial.* In denial, we lied to ourselves first; then we lied to others. We would drink and tell ourselves we would stop after one or two. Deep inside we knew this was a lie. Admitting is just speaking the truth. Our truth was that one or two never was enough for us; we wanted the high. We need honesty to recover. The Big Book says that those who do not recover are people who cannot or will not be honest with themselves.

In the First Step, we admitted alcohol and other drugs had become more important than family, friends, or a Higher Power. We put our lives in danger. We were willing to do anything to protect our relationship with chemicals. This is what is meant by admitting we had lost control of our lives. The more honest we can be when working the First Step, the stronger our sobriety will be.

". . . we were powerless over alcohol —. . ."
This simply means alcohol and other drugs had the power. Power means to have control over others. To be powerless means to have *no* control over others. In the First Step we admit we had *no* control at all over alcohol and other drugs. They had the power; they made the choices.

How could this be? Alcohol and other drugs by themselves have little power. What is then meant when we say that we are powerless over them? *We use and we lose control over what will happen.*

- We don't want bad things to happen, but when we use, they do.
- We don't want to hurt our families, but when we use, we do.
- We don't want to put our jobs and careers on the line, but when we use, often we do.

Also, we don't want to hurt ourselves. We hate pain just the way everyone else does. But when we use, we hurt ourselves. We are powerless. We use and we take on the mind of an addict. We lose our values and take on "addict values." We are powerless to stop this; we are hooked.

We might have told ourselves, "It's time to stop," but the alcoholic in us kept right on drinking. We had lost all power; we *couldn't* stop.

We might have told ourselves, "Don't treat your family this way," but the addict inside us laughed and kept on hurting them and *us.* We lost our power to choose.

It is said that the main thing that separates humans from animals is the power to make choices. Didn't we, at times, feel less than human? If anyone stood between us and our drinking or other drug use, we would fight and argue until we got what we wanted. Did we truly want to? Looking back with sober eyes, we say, "no." We wanted happiness just like everyone else. But we were sick and we acted the way addicts do. We hated the guilt we felt — it kept us human, but it also drove us back to using. The First Step is saying that if we use, we have no choice but to hurt ourselves and others.

By admitting we are powerless, we can now solve our problem. Honestly *admitting our problem* created the *answer* to our problem. If we have a problem we seek help. If we are chemically dependent, we seek out those who can help us free ourselves of addiction. Honesty opens the door for help. Admitting we're powerless will allow us to be free again. It gives us back the power to choose.

". . . that our lives had become unmanageable."

"What does this mean? I still had my job. Doesn't that mean my life was still manageable?" Many of us hate to admit our lives had become unmanageable. We wanted to prove we could manage instead of looking at how unmanageable our lives had become. It is as if a tornado had ripped apart our house, destroying everything except for one room. As addicts, we try to convince ourselves and everyone else that the house is in good shape because this one room is left.

Step One is saying there was a cost to us and others for our drinking and other drug use. This is what is meant by our lives being "unmanageable":

- Our families got hurt and angry because of our use.
- We felt ashamed because of our use.
- We might have wrecked cars.
- We didn't keep promises, we drank or used instead.
- Maybe we cheated on taxes and the time we put in at work.
- We pretended there was no cost to us or others due to our chemical use. This was the biggest lie. For drug dependencies there is *always* a cost.

Addiction keeps taking from our lives without putting anything of real value back into them. Addiction keeps taking and taking from us, our friends, and family. The First Step asks us to admit what our addiction has cost us. What was the price tag for our use? Feelings, spirit, body . . . and in terms of relationships, what were the costs?

The more honest we are about how unmanageable our lives have become the more respect we will have for the power of our illness. Alcoholism and drug dependency are powerful illnesses. The more honest we are in our self-examination the more we will see the need to reach outside of ourselves for help.

This is where Step Two comes in, so let's move on to it. A new way of life is now open to us.

STEP TWO

Came to believe that a Power greater than ourselves could restore us to sanity.

Step Two is a Step of hope. It is a clear statement that the insanity of our addiction can be taken from us. It means that much of the fear, confusion, anger, shame, worry, and sadness that our addiction created can be taken from us. It means our thinking can and will return to normal. All this adds up to hope.

Though we'll really want to feel sane again, most of us will resist Step Two. Many of us will say, "I wasn't really insane." If this is happening to you, it often means you need to spend more time with Step One. A complete First Step leaves no doubt that we were insane.

We can ask ourselves, *Do I believe I was insane?* Just because we were able to do things in some areas of our lives doesn't mean we were not insane. Sanity is defined as "soundness of judgment and reason." By the time we start working Step Two, we should clearly know our judgment and reasoning were not sound. When it came to making choices, we made bad choices.

- We chose alcohol or other drugs over our family.
- We chose alcohol or other drugs over health.
- We chose alcohol or other drugs over jobs, friends, schooling, and self-care.

The list goes on. In fact, because of our illness, we lost our ability to choose in any sane manner. This is what made us slaves. "Oh, I had choices," we might say. But when we honestly look back we see we had no choice. This was our insanity.

Maybe we were able to keep ourselves together at work. This was only because our disease had not gotten bad enough to wreck work *yet.* If it had, we would have chosen chemical use over our job. Whatever our addiction asked for, we gave it.

Others of us will resist Step Two because it sounds "religious." Many of us don't know the difference between religion and spirituality. The Steps or our groups are *not* religion in any sense of the word. But the Steps and our groups are very spiritual.

The Steps are about *healing our spirits* and *improving our relationship with our Higher Power.* Each person who uses the Twelve

Steps to get clean and sober will be asked to find and believe in a Higher Power. But it is up to each of us to define this Higher Power in our own way. There is no one right way to believe. In fact, there is no one right way to work the Steps.

Step Two keeps going where Step One left off — we must reach outside of ourselves. We must reach out to a Power greater than ourselves. As we work the Second Step, we will feel more of our loneliness leaving us. We will feel lighter and freer. Hope will again become part of our daily lives. We will watch help come to us in many forms. Step Two tells us to find a healing Power that will take care of us and comfort us. Let us now look at each part of Step Two.

"Came to believe . . ."

"Came to believe" means giving ourselves time. To truly believe means to wrestle with the parts of us that don't believe. We are not to be sheep and just say we believe — we are to take the time we need and *come* to believe.

There is a good booklet on this. It is called, *Surrender Versus Compliance in Therapy.*[1] Compliance means just going along with something because you are supposed to. In compliance, a part of us never really gives in.

In surrender, we struggle and work with and through the issue. Struggle is a part of recovery.

The major way addicts struggle is to deny the truth. If we've worked a good First Step, we see the insanity of struggling to deny our illness. We see the insanity of struggling to keep active something as dangerous to us as our drug dependence. We are to surrender, to give in and learn how to live *with* it.

Therefore, in recovery we give in to the fact that we are dependent on alcohol or other drugs and learn to live *with* this reality. In this way, Step Two is a Step about giving in and surrendering to our need for help. By giving in, the healing begins. In fact, in Step Two we are asked to believe we can be healed. We are asked to come to believe in a Power that can heal.

---

[1] Tiebout, Harry M., *Surrender Versus Compliance in Therapy* (Center City, Minn.: Hazelden Educational Materials). Reprinted by permission from Quarterly Journal of Studies on Alcohol, 1953.

Our addictions taught us not to trust. "Came to believe" means to trust. Will we trust again? In our addiction, we ended up trusting our addiction and only our addiction. We would put down other people who were doing well; we didn't trust them. We believed in only our addiction and nothing else.

The problem here is that putting our trust in our addiction led us to insanity, not to sanity. In Step Two, we are asked to start to believe in and trust a *positive* healing power. For us, believing in positives can be very hard. This is not good or bad; it is just a result of our illness.

So Step Two takes time. We give ourselves time — time to heal, time to believe again. Believing takes time. We don't just *say* we believe; we *come* to believe.

A number of us enter recovery ready to believe in a healing power. In fact, many come into the program looking for this. Why? Because the pain of our addiction is too much for us to handle. Many of us come into the program feeling and believing that we are crazy. We don't want to hurt others, but we keep doing this. We feel crazy in this way; thus Step Two is a welcome relief. It is the help we have been seeking.

We know we acted insane and we've wanted to believe there was hope. But nothing seemed to work. We became angry and hard. Or we became sad and depressed. People spoke of hope and love and we secretly laughed at them. We saw them as simple. We thought we had learned there was really nothing but ourselves to believe in. We had come to believe in despair. All hope had left us. We were bitter.

Step Two says *believe.* To believe is to have hope. We come to believe. How?

- We come to believe because we see the program and the Steps working for others.
- We see others who were as bad off or worse off than we were, and they got better. We see them happy and full of hope.

It is through others we will again come to believe. We need to see and be with other recovering people so we can again believe and know there is hope — there is recovery.

". . . Power greater than ourselves . . ."

As addicts, we know a lot about powers greater than ourselves. As we got sicker and sicker, we came to believe in nothing but alcohol and other drugs. We failed to see that a power greater than ourselves was now controlling our lives. This power was called alcoholism or chemical dependency.

All illnesses are powers greater than ourselves. They take us over. They get control. Our illness tricked us into believing we were getting our needs met when the truth is we were avoiding our troubles.

Step Two says we are to believe in a Power — a healing power — greater than ourselves. This Power does have to meet one very important condition: it must be able to restore us to sanity. We are to believe in health, in healing, and in hope.

Step Two does not say what this Power should be.

- It may be the Steps. They surely hold a Power greater than ourselves.

- It may be an A.A. or N.A. group. The group clearly is a Power that can help heal us.

- It may be God as we understand Him. God is clearly a Power greater than ourselves.

We will not be put down or kicked out if what we believe is different from the person next to us. The only question asked will be, "Does what you believe in hold the power to restore you to sanity?"

". . . could restore us to sanity."

In this part of Step Two, we find a key word: "could." This doesn't say "will" restore us to sanity; it says, "could" restore us to sanity. Thus, something is missing. What is missing will be found in the Third Step. We will be asked to do something. We will be asked to form a relationship with this Power.

This Power will give us sanity, but we will be asked to give in to it. In this way we learn about give and take. Addiction takes and takes and takes. It gives nothing to us without taking first. As we learn about give and take, we learn how to have a relationship that will work. The first real relationship we form in the program is with

13

this Power greater than ourselves that can, if used, restore us to sanity.

As stated earlier, sanity is soundness of judgment and reason. This is what will be restored to us — soundness of judgment and reason. What a gift! Again, we will be able to think clearly. We will be able to see the world as it truly is and not how our addiction wants us to see it.

Let us now move on to Step Three and see what we must give to this Power to have it heal us.

STEP THREE

Made a decision to turn our will and our lives over to the care of God as we understood Him.

In Step Two, we looked at our soundness of mind. Here in Step Three, we start to deal with our spirit. Chemical dependency is often called a spiritual disease. Because of our crazy relationship with alcohol and other drugs, we lost touch with the spiritual side of ourselves. Also, we became unable to find ways to connect with the spiritual side of others. Over time, we became lost spiritually; we became lonely inside. Our addiction starved us spiritually.

It was as if there was a wall built around us. No one could touch us, and we could touch no one. We had turned our lives over to alcohol and other drugs. They had become a power greater than ourselves. They always came first. We gave to our addiction whatever it asked — our self-respect, our relationships. Why?

The answer is simple: we had lost control. We had become, as the Big Book says, "self-will run riot." We only thought of me-me-me. We thought the high was what we wanted. We thought it brought us relief. It did not.

We wanted to be in control partly because we felt so out of control. Our addiction helped us believe we were in control. But this was a lie; we were *out* of control. We ended up having to have everything our own way. We didn't care who got hurt. By living this way, we became unsafe to others and ourselves. People started protecting themselves and their "spirit" when they were around us.

We also had to protect our own "spirit." We were unsafe and were hurtful to ourselves. So, slowly over time, we built a wall around our spirit and put it away, hoping for a time that it would be safe to bring it out again.

We also stopped doing things that made our *spirit* happy. Instead of loving others and connecting with them, we started staying away from others — except for our friends who drank or used.

- Instead of loving our spouse, we put him or her down.
- Instead of playing with our kids, we lectured them until we drove them away.

We put distance between our spiritual selves and the spirits of those who loved us. We stopped believing in others and ourselves. We went wherever our addiction took us. There was little care in our lives. We made a decision and turned our will and lives over to the pain of our addiction.

Step Three is wonderful. It's all about *care*. We are to turn our will and lives over to the care of God. We are to learn to act with care. The true beauty of the Third Step is in the order it will give to our lives.

Often we wonder, *Should I do this or not?* The Third Step gives us an easy way to answer these types of questions. When faced with a problem, we have to choose how to handle it. We ask ourselves, *What is the most caring way I can solve this?*

When we think of choices, we ask ourselves, *Would my Higher Power see my choice as one of care?* If the answer is "yes," we do it. If the answer is "no," then we don't do it. If the answer is "I'm not sure," then we wait until we know. As we wait, we talk with our friends and sponsor, asking them, "Do you believe my Higher Power would see this as an act of caring?" We are not lost anymore.

Whenever we come to a fork in the road, we choose the direction marked "care." Even if the road looks rougher and longer, we choose the direction marked "care." If we feel like putting down a family member, we ask ourselves, *Would this be seen as an act of caring?* If the answer is "no," we must look for another way to act. We are forced to grow. We are forced to find new ways of behaving. Step Three will continue to give us direction for the rest of our lives.

Let us look at the different parts that make up the Third Step.

"Made a decision . . ."

These words are very important for us. They speak to us of *choice.* We choose to work the Third Step. It will not happen by accident. Spirituality is about choice.

We don't become spiritual just because we stop drinking and taking other drugs. It is possible for our lives to naturally get better just by our stopping the act of putting poison into our bodies. But this doesn't mean our spirit will naturally get better. For this to happen, we must make a decision. Spirituality is chosen. Spiritual people *choose* to be spiritual people. The First and Second Steps gave us back the gift of choice; now it is up to us how we use it.

Choice makes us responsible for ourselves. Each time we look back and remind ourselves that we've made a decision to turn our will and lives over to the care of God, we become more responsible. Choice teaches us we have power — the power to choose or not to choose.

To make a decision means we start to take our power back. Our illness had stolen our power — our power to choose. We could not choose to drink or use — we just did. We wanted to stop, but we had no power. In Step Three we choose to bring our power back into our lives.

"Responsible" means *I am my actions and I am my choices.* During our addiction, we were irresponsible. We were trying to get others and ourselves to believe *I'm not responsible for my actions, and I have no choice.* Step Three helps us to become responsible for ourselves. We are responsible for our choices.

". . . to turn our will and lives over to the care of God . . ."

For many of us, this is the scariest part of the whole Twelve Step program. If we turn over our will and let go of our lives, who will run them? Is there really a God? Even if there is a God, why should I turn my life over when it's mine?

These are questions we all struggle with. Because of our illness we trusted no one and nothing. We trusted only alcohol and other drugs.

We struggle to trust. We may have to go back and struggle with the Second Step again. This is okay. We are not very trusting people. We believed in and still struggle with believing only in the "quick fix." We want control. We want that relief and we want it *now.*

In many ways this is the core of our illness: lack of trust, little faith. Our illness got started when we wanted to feel good. This is natural. We felt good, and, at least in the beginning, we felt relief when we used. But it never lasted, and none of our problems got solved.

The Third Step will give us a different kind of pleasure than we ever received from alcohol or another drug.

- We will get pleasure from not having to be in control. We will get pleasure from learning how to resolve our problems. Our lives will have direction and meaning again.
- We will get pleasure from the caring relationship we build with our Higher Power.
- We will get pleasure from trusting others, and from being able to trust ourselves.

Step Three will give us what we have been looking for all along — peace of mind.

We know we have turned our will and life over to the care of God when we stop worrying all the time about outcomes. Remember how we tried to control the outcomes we wanted? We would do anything to get our way. Step Three says *stop.* We are to turn our will and lives over to God. God will worry about the outcomes. God will give us the outcomes we need. So relax. Our job is to keep believing and trusting. The program says, "Let go, and let God."

We have turned our will and our lives over to the care of God. In life, horrible things do happen. There are accidents. Loved ones die. Step Three says our Higher Power and its care will help us through hard times. If we turn our will and lives over, we will get the care we need to survive and to heal. We turn our lives over to a caring and loving God.

Working the Third Step means that we make choices based on care. We look for care (not pleasure) and head that way because that is where we will find our Higher Power.

". . . as we understood Him."

You don't have to believe in God to work Step Three. You can define and understand God in any way you want. Maybe your definition of God is a Power greater than yourself that can restore you to sanity (Step Two), and this Power cares about you (Step Three). Many people, whether or not they believe in God, use the term "Higher Power." For them, their group could be their Higher Power because it provides them with care. Many define Nature as their loving, healing Higher Power. It is up to you to decide. No one else can tell you how to define God; you have your own personal relationship with your Higher Power.

Step Three needs to be worked throughout each day. Because life is full of decisions, we need to keep in mind what our Higher Power would want for us. We need to think about the Third Step whenever we face a choice. After awhile, choosing care will become a way of life.

Once we have turned our will and lives over to the care of our Higher Power, we are ready to take on another task for the program. We are to look inside ourselves. We are now ready to work on Step Four.

STEP FOUR

Made a searching and fearless moral inventory of ourselves.

As we work the first three Steps, we come to understand more and more about just how ill we were because of our addiction. We understand how our illness changed us into different people. Hopefully, we will be different people because of our recovery.

While we were ill, we were so full of shame we didn't want to look at ourselves. We hated the thought of it.

- It hurt us to look at ourselves and think we were unable to change.
- It hurt to see how unmanageable our lives had become.
- It made us sad to see how out of control we had become.

To look at ourselves meant to look squarely into the eyes of our addiction. This was a painful thing to do. For this reason, we developed great skills of denial. We could deny anything, especially if it had to do with our drug dependency. It would have been too hard to see ourselves through honest eyes. So, we looked the other way and became dishonest.

The Fourth Step is designed to help us come to know ourselves again. We are forced to stop and look at ourselves. We become honest again. Honesty means we must see ourselves as responsible. But to do so we must first know who we are. We also need to come to know the addict personality inside of ourselves. For this reason, the Fourth Step can be a bit painful at times, as all growth can be.

Through working a Fourth Step we will be able to understand both our good and bad sides. We humans have what it takes to be good and what it takes to be bad. This comes with choice. We will need to accept this and work to better understand ourselves and the choices we make. Because we hurt ourselves and others with our dishonesty, our illness was able to grow. To keep a sober lifestyle, we will need to be able to look at ourselves honestly. The Fourth Step teaches us this important skill.

In ancient Greece, the spiritual center of the country was found in an area called Delphi. At Delphi, seven wise people got together and boiled all the wisdom of the time into two simple phrases that were then cut into the entry to their temple. The first was,

"NOTHING TO EXCESS." The second was, "KNOW THY SELF."
The Fourth Step is about this. Through the Fourth Step we will get to know ourselves, all of ourselves, the good, the bad, the ugly, and the beautiful.

Let us now look in depth at the Fourth Step and its different parts.

"Made a searching and fearless . . ."

When we take an inventory of ourselves we should be very complete. This is what is meant by "searching." We are not to do just a surface inventory. We are to look deep inside of ourselves and see who and what we are truly made of. We are to push ourselves to look deep inside to see what we became as we acted out our addiction.

After we do a Fourth Step, we should have a clear picture of what and who we would become if we were to start using again. We should have a clear picture of who we hurt, and how, during our drinking and drug-using years (this will help later in doing Steps Eight and Nine).

We are to look at *all* of our values and beliefs and ask ourselves questions such as, "Do I like this belief or value?" or "Is it helpful to me and others?" or "Is this my belief or is it a product of my illness?"

If we find something we don't like we have to honestly ask, "Can I change it or for some reason has this behavior or attitude become important to me?" We may not want to get rid of or give up all of our character defects. At this time, it is very important and very hard to be honest. It is here the term "fearless" comes into play.

We must not turn away and deny some part of ourselves or some behavior just because of our fear. Being fearless doesn't mean that we're never afraid. The Fourth Step is a very scary task. Being fearless means we don't let our fear stop us. We look at all sides of who we are and how we have acted.

Doing a Fourth Step is also an act of faith. We put our fears to the side and believe our Higher Power will provide us with enough care to be able to do this difficult task.

Our illness was based on our not having a clear picture of who we were. We were ill because we were afraid of knowing ourselves. Thus, the Fourth Step gives us the skills to search out and build a clear picture of who we are. We do not let our fears get in our way. If they start to, we now have a support system. We can talk about the fears and continue our inventory. It is through our support system that our Higher Power will provide us with love and support.

". . . moral inventory . . ."

What the heck does "moral" mean? Does it sound hard? Does it sound as though we might end up with a lot of shame? Well, parts of the Steps are hard and this is a hard part. Moral means, "Having to do with right and wrong." In the Fourth Step, we are to make a list of what is right and what is wrong about us. This is hard, but necessary work.

The Little Red Book states, "The purpose of taking a moral inventory is to expose the harmful character traits of our alcoholic personalities, to eliminate [get rid of] them."[2] The program says we need to know what parts make up the addict inside of us so we can grow beyond them. Thus, we look squarely and honestly at our addiction.

In the Fourth Step, we can sit down with paper and pencil and write our inventory. To do a complete inventory will take time. We have much to go over. Be fair and give yourself this time. Fourth Step guide booklets can be helpful in getting us started. Often, our sponsor will know where we can get these. Our intergroup associations often have booklets on the subject.[*] Remember, we are now people who seek out and accept help in all forms. We are not loners anymore.

The true gift of the Fourth Step is that we get to know ourselves again. We need to know ourselves and gain a complete picture of ourselves. As we learned in the First Step, we have to first admit what is wrong before we can change anything.

In listing the rights and wrongs of how we have behaved, we learn about what we believe in and what we value.

For example, we may find out something like, *I often lie to my spouse about money.* Then we have to ask ourselves, *Do I put too much importance on money?* Maybe we learn that inside we feel very small but we used money to come across as a big shot to cover this up. Maybe we find out that we drink to help cover up

---

[2] *The Little Red Book* (Center City, Minn.: Hazelden Educational Materials, 1970), 57.
[*] Hazelden Educational materials has many guides available in its catalog.

this feeling of being small. If so, then we know we'll need to share these findings with our support system.

Remember, this is a ''moral inventory'' having to do with right and wrong. We need to be as honest with what is right about ourselves as we are about what is wrong. Again, we are looking for a clear and complete picture of ourselves. There is a lot right about us too!

Remember when we hurt about the way we acted? This guilt speaks to the good inside of us that was not let out because of our illness. For some of us, making a moral inventory about what is right with us will be a lot harder than listing what is wrong. Shame had become an old friend. A lot of us just surrendered to our addiction and came to think of ourselves as bad people. This is how we explained the way we acted.

If this is the case with you, then you will need to spend more time getting to know and accept the good inside of you.

As we take our inventory, we come to see ourselves in a more balanced way. We are both good and bad. We are the beauty; we are the beast. We need to see ourselves in this balanced way.

We need to step back and look at ourselves with honesty, but with an open attitude. We are not perfect, and this is okay. We are humans, and humans are both good and bad. If you doubt this, pick up a newspaper. Inside you will find stories of the bad and sometimes horrible things humans do, and you will find stories of the beautiful and wonderful things humans do. In our addiction we tried to hide what was wrong with us. Through the Fourth Step we learn to look at ourselves for who we truly are.

There is one small but important part of the Fourth Step we need to look at. The last two words of the Fourth Step are. . .

''. . . of ourselves.''

The Fourth Step is very clear. We take inventories of *ourselves.* We don't take inventories for our friends. We don't do inventories for family members. We do inventories for *ourselves.*

In addiction, we often blamed others for how we felt inside. Through the Fourth Step, we get the focus back where it belongs — on ourselves.

Once we have done a Fourth Step inventory, we are ready to move on to Step Five. Let's do that now.

STEP FIVE

Admitted to God, to ourselves, and to another human being the exact nature of our wrongs.

So far we have admitted we have an illness. We have found and come to believe there is help for us. We have given up control and decided to let our Higher Power run our lives. We have taken time out and done an inventory of just what type of person we had become due to our illness.

Now we are on the move once again. We have our inventories and now it is time to do something with them. In Step Five we are able to take the part of our inventory that has to do with our wrongs and share them with God, ourselves, and another person.

Why? Why would we want to tell anyone about them? Why does the program have us do this instead of taking our inventories and burying them somewhere or burning them? Why do we have to let others know about our addictive personalities?

We are to do this because it goes against everything that is addictive inside of us. As addicts, we kept all of this secret. Honesty, especially public honesty, was something we never took part in. But honest statement of who we truly are is a basic need all human beings have. By honestly talking about our alcoholic and drug dependent personalities, we gain what the program calls "humility." Humility is the ability to see the world and ourselves as we truly are. Humility is a key to staying sober.

The Fifth Step is designed to start us talking about our wrongs. As we talk and share our wrongs with God, ourselves, and someone else, they will have less power over us. The Fifth Step is a way for us to get some distance from the shame that our addiction has created inside of us. Shame is a very powerful force. Shame is that painful feeling that rises up inside of us when we go against our values and hurt ourselves or someone else.

The Fifth Step will also help free us from our false pride. Step Five prepares us for future Steps when we'll have to talk to the people we've harmed and try to set things right. Through the Fifth Step and the other Steps, we become moral people again.

By talking to someone else about the wrongs we have done during our alcohol and drug-using days, we are making firm our new conscience. We are telling someone else we know these things were wrong. In the past, we pretended that we did no wrong. We pretended that we didn't know right from wrong. We blamed others for the ways we acted and refused to lay claim to our wrongs. The Fifth Step says we are to admit to our wrongs.

Let's now look at this Step in more detail.

"Admitted to God, to ourselves, and to another human being . . ."

The Fifth Step, more than any other Step so far, has us reaching outside of ourselves. In this way the Fifth Step is a Step about connection. We are to take our program outside of ourselves. We are to connect with our Higher Power. We are to connect with ourselves, and we are to connect with another human being. This is a new element.

Our program is not just between ourselves and our Higher Power. In order for us to work our program, we have to talk to another person about our addictive personalities. Our private, often shameful secrets, will be out. Someone else will know just how mean we can get.

- We will talk about our dishonesty, anger, and resentments.
- We will also talk about how fearful we were and how jealous and how critical we were of others.
- We are to tell all.
- We are to tell about how we hurt our families.
- We are to describe the looks on their faces as we yelled at them for daring to tell us we had a drinking or other drug problem.

For the first time in our lives, we are to be totally honest with another person.

Because this is not an easy task, it is not a Step to rush into. For most of us there will come a time when we want to tell all and have everything out in the open. We want to be free of our past lives and all of our painful memories. We want to get on with our lives.

Sometimes, we secretly don't want the relief Step Five can bring. We want to punish ourselves for our past behavior. We want to see ourselves as different and bad people. If this is the case with you, then do a Fifth Step now. You deserve the relief.

In Step Five, we share first with our Higher Power. We talk to our Higher Power as we would anyone else, telling of all the things we have done wrong. We see our Higher Power as a Power we can have a close relationship with, as a friend. Some may call this prayer. Others just call it talking. It doesn't matter. Through the care of God, we will come to find a way to forgive ourselves for the ways we acted and the attitudes we developed during our addiction.

Next, we share with ourselves about our wrongs. This is very important. We are to let ourselves see and have feelings about the ways we acted. This is the way we develop a conscience. We develop a sense of right and wrong *within* ourselves. The more we let our conscience direct our lives, the more it can bring us comfort.

We are learning about self-respect in sharing with ourselves. We are building a relationship with the part of us that has values we can believe in. In this part of the Fifth Step, we start to define our personal values and thus gain self-respect. As we work the Fifth Step, we will find that we do have beliefs and values about how we should treat others.

The pain we feel as we work this Step is partly from gaining information about what we believe is important. So if we find ourselves shedding a tear or two as we talk to ourselves, we need to see this as self-knowledge about what we believe to be wrong. They are tears of conscience. We are healing.

Next, and most likely the hardest, is that we share our wrongs with another human being. This is hard. We are to tell all to another person. Because of this, we need to choose this person carefully. It needs to be someone we trust. We need to trust that the person will not tell others what we have shared with him or her. It can be anyone we trust, who is willing to hear our Fifth Step. Because of the type of things most of us share in our Fifth Step, many people choose a clergyperson to hear their Fifth Step. Many clergy have had special training in hearing Fifth Steps.

The book *Alcoholics Anonymous* has much to say on the topic of the Fifth Step. The first four pages of Chapter Six are about the Fifth Step. You may want to read this. The one thing the book stresses is that we are to *tell all*. Because we have led this secret life, we need to finally have someone hear it all. We also need to hear ourselves tell someone all we can remember.

Alcoholics Anonymous also tells us what we are to do after telling someone our Fifth Step. It says, "Returning home we find a place where we can be quiet for an hour, carefully reviewing what we have done. We thank God from the bottom of our heart that we know Him better . . . we ask if we have omitted [left out] anything, for we are building an arch through which we shall walk a free person at last."[3]

This arch is made up of our Higher Power, ourselves, and others. At last, we will again have the skills to form relationships that work. We can leave all the shame behind.

We get all this by our sharing. What do we share? We are to share . . .

". . . the exact nature of our wrongs."

The Fifth Step is very clear. We are to share exactly what it is we did wrong and why it was wrong. We don't share a general statement like, "I was selfish during my drinking." We share *exactly* how we were selfish, such as, "I stole money from my spouse so I could go out and drink." We don't beat around the bush. We don't make excuses. We just share the exact nature of our wrongs.

We do this to help ensure that we will not drink or use again. We don't want any secrets sitting around that we can feel guilty and shameful about. We also do it because it is humbling and we need all the humility we can get. Humility is a building block to sobriety.

Often, the type of wrongs we may want to hold back from sharing in our Fifth Step are the very things we feel the worst and most shameful about. It is these wrongs that are most likely to get us drunk or using again. The wrongs that we don't want anyone to know about have a habit of popping up at the times we feel most like drinking or using. Thus, it is very important that we tell all in our Fifth Step.

We need to keep in mind that we are fighting for our lives. We can't risk our lives to protect any part of our using history. We have much to do in our new lives and we need to get rid of all the

---

[3] *Alcoholics Anonymous* (New York: A.A. World Services, Inc., 1976), 75.

garbage from the past. Hopefully, we will feel lighter and freer after doing a Fifth Step.

Let's now move on to Step Six for help in removing our defects of character.

STEP SIX

Were entirely ready to have God remove all these defects of character.

Because of Steps Four and Five, we are now changed people. We will never see our lives the same way we used to. These Steps have led us to see ourselves in a new and different light. For the first time in years, we now know ourselves in a more complete way. We won't like everything we see, and we'll want to change. But there is one more bit of recovery we must do before we can change the things we don't like about ourselves. We must become ready for the changes. We must take Step Six.

When we work on Step Six, we build on the work we did in Steps Four and Five. When we were using our mood-changing chemicals, we often lived in a world of "let's pretend." If we didn't like some part of our personality, we would pretend it wasn't there, or blame it on someone else. So we needed Steps Four and Five to help us see who we truly are, with all our good points as well as our bad points.

We have worked very hard on Step Four to get to know ourselves.

In Step Five we took responsibility for who we are by admitting to God, to ourselves, and to another human being what we have learned about ourselves.

In Step Six, we will find that becoming entirely ready to have God remove these defects of character is quite a process in itself.

"Were entirely ready . . ."

What is meant by this? The founders of this program were both honest and realistic people. They knew that we, as addicts, are impulsive people — we want quick and easy fixes, and we tend to act before we think things through. The founders also knew that quick and easy answers don't last — "easy come, easy go." So in writing Step Six, they were saying, in a sense, "Slow up and think. This is serious stuff."

At first, we don't realize how much change we are in for when our character defects are removed. We think things will be pretty easy without the crummy parts of our behavior. But our character defects are deeply rooted, and we are attached to them. In fact, we grew to depend on our character defects. We were comfortable with them. They seemed natural and normal to us. We believed in our defects. We believed we needed them.

We were selfish people, and believed that we needed our selfishness. We thought everyone was selfish and we would be fools to give it up. If we didn't look out for Number One, who would?

The founders of this program knew how people change. To change, even for the better, takes time. We need time to become "entirely ready." Step Six is a getting-ready Step. Getting ready is action. This is not a Step to pass over lightly. It is often a Step that is overlooked because many of us have a hard time understanding that getting ready means action and hard work.

It might help to think of Step Six as being similar to getting ready to plant a garden in our yard. Having a good garden takes a lot of work before the first seed ever gets planted. First, we have to look over the yard to find a good spot. We check out how much sunlight hits that spot, and what kind of soil is there. Then we plan what we want to plant, making sure we have the tools, fertilizer, and seeds. Next, we wait for the right time of year, then we roll back the sod, cultivate the soil, pick out the rocks, fertilize, and plan the rows. *Now* we are ready to plant the seed!

Having our defects of character removed also takes a lot of preparation. First, we look ourselves over in Step Four, and we admit who we are in Step Five. Then we start thinking about changing in Step Six.

Since we tuned into them, we start to see our character defects pop up all over. The first thing we want to do when we see our crummy behavior come out over and over is pretend it isn't happening. We find ourselves in denial again, just like our denial of chemical dependency. Why? Because it makes us feel bad to see how often our character defects come out in our behavior. We feel shame. We judge ourselves as being bad. So we hide our bad behavior from ourselves just like we hid our chemical dependency from ourselves.

We have to stop feeling shame about our character defects before we can change. Why? Because our shame keeps us from seeing them honestly and learning from them. We must accept and love ourselves even when we clearly see how we are not perfect. Then we are free to look at our defects and learn from them.

As we start to see our character defects in action more and more, we get to know them better. We see *when* we use them. We see *what happens* to us and to other people when we use them. It hurts us to see the ways we hurt ourselves and others with our character defects, because we want to be recovering, loving, and fair people.

We talk about our defects with others who understand. We think and meditate about our defects. We ask ourselves:

- *Why do I act that way?*
- *What will happen when I stop acting that way?*
- *How would I like to act instead?*

We are preparing. We are getting ready to let Step Six help us to accept ourselves with dignity. Our self-respect should be returning. As we work Step Six, we should start to feel true humility.

Humility means we have an honest view and open attitude about who we are and how we fit into the world. We accept both our good and bad sides without giving in to self-pity or shame.

Our self-pity was a sign that we were not taking responsibility for doing something about our character defects.

Our shame was a sign that we were not willing to see ourselves for who we were. We thought that if we did, we would judge ourselves as being bad people.

We aren't ready to change until we take a humble look at ourselves. It takes a certain amount of healing before we can ask to be changed. Through working Steps Four and Five, we see and admit that we are only human. We can do both good and bad. In working Step Six, we go one step further — we *accept* ourselves, just as we are. If we are still feeling shameful about some of our behaviors, we may need to work on them by talking more with a friend, our sponsor, a clergyperson, a counselor, or all of these. By doing this, we are working Step Six. We are *preparing* ourselves to have these defects of character removed. One of the main ways we get ready for the removal of our defects is through honest acceptance of them as part of us.

For many of us, Step Six can often sound more like a question than a statement. We say we're entirely ready, but we hear the questioning in our voice. *Am I really ready to live without them? Am I really ready to live in a different way?*

This questioning is normal. It's because we question that there is a need for Step Six. Again, we need time to truly become ready to give up our character defects.

So allow yourself time to work with Step Six. Read about it. Talk with your Twelve Step group about it. Talk with your sponsor, but most of all allow yourself the time needed to become "entirely ready."

". . . to have God remove . . ."

As we begin to see our problem behaviors in action, we go through the stage of trying to control our behavior. We make promises to ourselves and to others. "I'll never do that again," we say, and we mean it. But we find ourselves doing it again.

Sometimes we don't do or say *exactly* the same thing again — we put a new little twist on it to fool ourselves. Bit by bit, we see that we can't change many of our personality problems and crummy behaviors. We need help once more.

This Step states clearly who is going to remove our character defects. Our Higher Power, God as we understand Him, will be the one to remove our defects of character. Step Six reminds us of our dependence on our Higher Power. Step Six reminds us of our need for a strong relationship with our Higher Power.

For most of us, giving up our character defects and letting someone help us is hard. We were loners who believed we could handle everything on our own. Through our program of recovery, though, we are starting to trust that it works to ask for help from our Higher Power. In meetings, we watched others change. We've seen a loving, caring God heal people and help them become the people they've wanted to be all along. We've watched God in action.

Our Higher Power will remove our defects of character if we stay connected to people. Our Higher Power works through people. Spirituality and the healing it brings comes from relationships with people — loving, caring relationships. We will need to find our Higher Power each day in the new relationships our recovery brings to us.

As we learn to have caring relationships, our character defects will be removed. Since God works through people, let's stay close to the people recovery has brought to us. We should treat our family members with as much care and respect as we do our new relationships. As we do this, our Higher Power will have many people to work through as He removes our character defects.

". . . all these defects of character."

Yes, *all* of our defects of character can be removed. In Step Six, we see the power found in the Twelve Steps. It clearly states, "all these defects of character." If we're ready, this Step promises they can be removed. This is the beauty of Step Six. It gives us hope. We can start to believe that we can be the people we now want to be.

We've been too angry. Step Six promises this can be removed. We've had too much self-pity. This can be removed. *All* our defects can be removed. All we have to do is prepare ourselves to live without them.

We've seen the miracles of the program happen right before our eyes. In our group, we've watched sad people become happy people. We've watched angry people turn into gentle people. We've watched controlling, pushy people become giving people. Step Six tells us that all we have to do to become one of these miracles is to become ready. To prepare. Once we've become "entirely ready," we are ready for Step Seven. Let's move on now and find out how to have these defects removed.

STEP SEVEN

Humbly asked Him to remove our shortcomings.

Step Seven will complete a journey we started back with Step Four. Because of Steps Four, Five, and Six, we now know ourselves in a more complete way. If we have worked these Steps without holding back, we will now be ready to humbly ask our Higher Power for help. We now know that we *need* help in removing our shortcomings, our defects of character. They are stumbling blocks to serenity in our lives.

Step Seven is a Step of prayer. Prayer is talking with our Higher Power. There is nothing special in the way we alcoholics and drug addicts pray. But Step Seven is a guide for us in how we are to pray. It says we are to *humbly* ask our Higher Power. Humility is defined by *The Little Red Book* as ''a true evaluation of conditions as they are; willingness to face facts, an understanding of the proper relationship between ourselves and a Higher Power and between ourselves and our fellowman.''[4]

We can now see the gift we've received from working Steps Four, Five, and Six is the gift of humility. Alcoholics and other drug addicts are not humble people by nature. Our illness stole our ability to clearly see ourselves and the world around us. Now in Step Seven, we are asked to use our newfound humility.

Humility means accepting and finding peace in our humanness. We aren't perfect, but we love ourselves anyway. During our addiction, we didn't want to accept ourselves as human, with human limits. We wanted to be perfect, and we wanted those around us to be perfect too. We pushed, pushed, and pushed some more, trying to be better than human. We denied our feelings, the most human part of us. We demanded our family and those around us do things in our crazy ways. We were ''always right.'' More and more, we put distance between ourselves and our human nature. We were anything but humble people.

Step Seven says we are to find the center of our humanness and pray to our Higher Power from there. Humility will become our strong suit.

---

[4] *The Little Red Book* (Center City, Minn.: Hazelden Educational Materials, 1970), 14.

- Instead of acting like know-it-all addicts, we will be humble.
- Instead of acting like self-pitying addicts, we will be humble.

We are to develop humility until it becomes a way of life for us.

Humility has nothing to do with weakness. In the past, we often believed that to be humble was to be weak. But that is not true. To be truly humble is the greatest strength a person can have. Why?

Because to be truly humble means to totally accept ourselves and those around us. It is to begin to see the world as it is. The pretending is gone.

- We begin to understand our strengths and weaknesses.
- We know we need others and that others need us.
- We start to feel balanced.
- We're not afraid that we'll be found out, because more and more, we are the same people wherever we go.
- We don't put on different masks as we move around in the world.
- We don't need to pretend so much.

A humble person knows there will be joy in life, but also knows there will be times of sadness, despair, anger, and grief. This is the way of the world.

People who are truly humble accept that they can't remove their shortcomings. Humility demands that we ask for help when we can't do something by ourselves. False pride tells us we must handle everything by ourselves; the humble person gladly seeks out help.

As you can see, Step Seven is an *action* Step. It is active; we take action. We are doing something. We humbly ask. In this way, Step Seven is like a mini Step Three. We again are turning something over to our Higher Power. In Step Three, it was our will and lives; in Step Seven, it is our shortcomings. We are admitting we can't rid ourselves of our shortcomings — that only our Higher Power can free us of them.

Let's now look at the parts of Step Seven.

"Humbly . . ."

Step Seven is talking about an attitude we are to have that will allow us to communicate with our Higher Power. We wouldn't *demand* Him to remove our shortcomings just as we wouldn't demand a friend to come over and help us. Thus, we are to *humbly* ask for help.

Most of us get humility and shame mixed up. Perhaps we resisted Step Seven because we thought that asking for help was a shameful thing to do. It is not. It is a free thing to do. Most of us thought that to be humble we had to become weak people who lack self-esteem and were afraid to stand up for anything. By working the Steps, especially Four, Five, and Six (that make up the complete inventory process), we develop a new understanding of what it means to be humble.

To be humble means to put aside our self-will. In our addiction, we became nothing *but* self-will, to the point that it was killing us and stopping us from having healthy relationships.

In Step Seven, we will ask that all of our self-will be removed. Why do we want our self-will removed? The main reason is so we can connect again with others. So we can build relationships. So we can be a helpful member of a family. So we can give more and take less.

Also we need our self-will removed so we can find our spiritual voice. Each of us has a spiritual voice within that guides us through life. In our illness, we learned not to listen to this voice — in fact, often we went directly against any good advice it gave us. Using our new humility to ask for our Higher Power's help will make our self-will less and help our spiritual voice get stronger.

". . . asked Him . . ."

This part of the Step is very clear. We are to ask. A hard task for us alcoholics and other drug addicts. But Step Seven won't work unless we ask. We are not to con, bargain, beg, demand, or manipulate our Higher Power to remove our shortcomings; we are to ask. We are to humbly ask for help.

Asking for help in a humble way is a necessary skill to have in life. Many of our troubles were due to the fact we couldn't ask for help. Our illness was lengthy because we couldn't admit that we had it and ask for help.

The gifts of Step Seven are not only that our shortcomings can be removed, but that we learn to ask for help. We learn how to *humbly* ask for help.

When we can't ask for help, we are blocked by a form of denial. It is dishonest. In working Step Seven, we are again asked to be honest about another part of our humanness — that is, all humans have needs they can't meet by themselves. We all have to be able to *ask* for help.

Again, the true gift of Step Seven is that it teaches us how to ask for what we need in a way that our needs can be met.

". . . to remove our shortcomings."

Step Seven speaks of removing our shortcomings. If we truly and humbly ask our Higher Power to remove our shortcomings, they will be removed. Many of us have the image that once we ask, *poof*, in a magical way, a cloud of smoke will rise up around us, and we'll be totally changed people from that moment on. That's our "quick fix" thinking. As addicts, we always think in terms of the quick fix. Because we could get high and change our moods in a matter of minutes, we believe that everything should work that fast.

For a few, Step Seven will change them totally and quickly. For most of us, if we work this Step our shortcomings will be removed, but on our Higher Power's time schedule, not on ours. Our Higher Power might not remove character defects until we have learned from them.

Step Seven is also about renewing our relationship with our Higher Power. By asking for help in the removal of our shortcomings, we must remember we are the major tool through which our Higher Power works. We should understand that we are agreeing to help our Higher Power remove our shortcomings. Our relationship with our Higher Power is a partnership. We work together.

Our Higher Power directs us and we do the work. The sole purpose of Step Seven is to help bring us closer to our Higher Power. The more we allow our Higher Power to help us, the closer our relationship will be. Step Seven binds us in a very complete way with our Higher Power.

One of the main ways we'll know that Step Seven is working is that the spiritual voice inside of us will be much clearer. The Seventh Step doesn't imply that we'll be perfect. It means that the voice of our Higher Power will be much clearer inside of us. Our conscience will be stronger. Thus, when we do think about a certain behavior, the spiritual voice inside of us will clearly ask,

"Do you really want to do this?" We will have more choices in our lives. God heals us by giving us choices and a conscience.

We've been healed in many ways as we've worked on our recovery with Steps One through Seven. Let's move on to the Step that helps us build and regain our relationship with family, friends, and the world around us — Step Eight.

STEP EIGHT

Made a list of all persons we had harmed, and became willing to make amends to them all.

Up to now, the Steps have had us working at rebuilding our relationship with our Higher Power and with ourselves. They have taught us a new way of life. The Steps have been creating new attitudes and beliefs inside of us. Now we should be living our lives using a new set of spiritual ideas. Now we will have developed a deeper relationship with our Higher Power. Spirituality has become a part of us, not just a nice idea. We are now ready for Step Eight.

In Step Eight we are back to facing our illness head on. In Step Eight we will be looking at the harm our illness has caused those around us. We will be looking at just how mean and cruel we can act when our illness controls us. Ours is a very cruel disease, not just to us, but to many other people. If addicts believe they have only hurt themselves, they are still very much wrapped up in addictive insanity.

Our illness affects mind, body, and soul. It also affects our relationships. As using addicts, we often had hurtful, mostly dishonest relationships. Dishonesty always hurts. To truly recover and start again, we will need to own up to the hurt and damage we have caused. Until we work Step Eight we can't leave the past behind us. We can't just overlook those we have harmed and used. To do this would be hurting them again.

Some of us may try to avoid this Step by saying, "It was because of my illness that I acted the way I did. I am not responsible for what I did." This is not true. Though we have an illness we are still responsible to live spiritual lives and to work our program. We have a responsibility to go back and try and fix any damage our illness has caused.

Like Step Six, Step Eight is a "getting ready" Step. One of the most important parts of Step Eight is getting an attitude of *willingness.* We are to take the time we need to become willing. Making amends when we aren't really sorry will not be helpful to us or to anyone else.

Step Eight, along with Step Nine, will help us correct past mistakes. It will help us get balance back into our relationships. But most of all, it will help us feel really clean again. After working these two Steps, we shouldn't be afraid to walk down any street and worry about who we may run into. Our slate will be clean.

In other words, much of the shame and hurt caused by our illness can be set right. We must be willing. This is why there is a separation between Step Eight and Step Nine. The main job in Step Eight is to develop the willingness to talk to people and try and set right *any* harm we may have done to *anyone.* We are to be willing to make amends to them *all.*

Let's now break Step Eight down into parts and look at what each holds.

"Made a list of all persons we had harmed, . . ."

In many ways this list should already have been made. If we've done a complete Fourth Step, our list should exist. Step Eight may be just going through the Fourth Step and pulling together a formal list.

Step Eight is very clear that we are to make a list. We are to get out paper and pen and put down in writing those we have harmed. This will make it more real. For this reason, some of us will want to avoid making the list. We may have said, "I'll have a mental list." This is too incomplete. Don't hedge or make light of this Step. We need to take very seriously the harm we have done to others. For us, the danger is that we may get drunk or use drugs if we try to avoid looking at the harm we have caused. Thus, we sit down and put together our list.

The Little Red Book suggests our list will be made up of four groups.

- Group One — friends. In this group, we will include ways we have harmed our close friends and any other people we would normally have had a good relationship with.

- Group Two — families. Most often, this is the group we have done the most damage to.

- Group Three — creditors. Often, our illness leads to money troubles. If this is the case, then anyone we owe money to or have stolen from should be put on the list.

- Group Four — the deceased. Often, because our illness has been long-standing, there are those we have harmed who are no longer living.

We need to make our list as complete as we possibly can for the moment. The longer we are in the program and the more we think about our lives, the more we'll remember. Thus, our list must always be open-ended, so we can add to it as we progress and become more honest.

The Little Red Book suggests we work out our amends with these people through our Higher Power. Through prayer and true willingness, these relationships can also be made clean.

We should always include ourselves on our list. We have harmed our bodies, our minds, and our spirits. So we will need to become willing to make amends to ourselves. Our amends to ourselves will be sobriety and good self-care. If we haven't been to a doctor in years, we should go to get a physical and then go regularly. If we haven't been to a dentist in years, go. And then go regularly. The proper amend to ourselves is regular attendance in A.A. and our groups, and taking good care of our bodies and our spirits.

". . . and became willing to make amends . . ."

This is the part of the Eighth Step that makes it a preparation Step. We are preparing to do Step Nine. We must keep in mind that preparing for a journey and the journey itself are two separate events. In Step Eight, we are to develop an attitude of willingness. We are to become willing to go out and try to set right any wrongs of our illness. Becoming willing can be the hardest part of Step Eight. It means giving up more self-will. This is true for many of the Steps.

Most people avoid Step Eight in two main ways: denial and resentments. In denial, a lot of us pretend we hurt no one but ourselves. If we are at this point, it may be best for us to spend time back on Steps One and Four. Or maybe we need to ask our family and friends what it was like for them during our using. If we do this, we need to be open to *listening* to others. We'll need to listen for the hurt and resentment of how our illness has affected them.

Resentments are mostly anger trapped by our self-will. We often want to look at our own hurt instead of admitting how we have hurt others. The truth is *we have been hurt, but Steps Eight and Nine are not about that.* The main work of Step Eight for many is to give up resentments.

41

We want to focus on our self-pity, on how we have been hurt, and say, "I'm not going to make amends until they say how they were wrong!" This is a good example of how we will hold on to our craziness. We'll need to change this around to complete Step Eight.

We'll need to say and believe, "Yes, that person hurt me, but for my sobriety I need to make amends." Step Eight is like Step Six because we're getting ready to throw out old garbage that we no longer need. This is especially important for us addicts because we have a habit of getting drunk or using drugs over old garbage. Resentments are old garbage.

Becoming willing is a very freeing experience. We feel more peaceful inside. We find ourselves having a clearer head and making better choices. Becoming willing frees us to have different types of relationships. Our relationships are now based on care and working through issues instead of trying to be the most powerful person. Making amends is about getting our relationships back on even ground.

During our addiction (and maybe still at times in recovery) our relationships were out of balance. Our relationships were unfair. Family and friends tried to connect with us, but instead ended up connected to our illness. Our resentment can keep this going.

To become willing, we need to give up our resentment. This doesn't mean that our anger and hurt are gone. It does mean we'll look at our part of the relationship and do something about it. The Eighth Step is for *us,* to help us become more spiritual and to reduce our chances of ever using again. We are to try; we are to admit the harm we've done. To develop willingness, we'll need to focus on our behavior toward others and not on their behavior toward us.

Sobriety is not enough, because sobriety alone will not make us spiritual people. We need to become spiritual people to stay sober and happy.

Step Eight is a Step that tests how much we are willing to stay happy and sober. Are we willing to give up hurt, defenses, and resentments? Are we willing to learn a state of mind that says, *If I hurt someone, no matter what the reason, I have a responsibility to correct that hurt?*

". . . to them all."

That's right! The Step says "to them all." We become willing to correct *all* past wrongs. This doesn't mean we'll get a chance to do so, face to face. But we are to find the part of us that is willing to correct all past wrongs.

The truth is, we don't *need* any of these past hurts and resentments. We are to get ready to make amends to anyone we have hurt. We may hate some people, but in Step Nine we'll be asked to make amends to them. So we need to work at becoming willing. This means a lot of talking in group, with program friends, and with our Higher Power.

The gift of Step Eight is that we learn how to take care of our spiritual needs even when we don't feel like it. As addicts, we did only as we wanted. Even if something was in our best interest, we may have felt like not doing it and avoided it. Step Eight says, "Sorry, find a way to do it." Spirituality comes before oneself. Relationships come before self-centeredness.

Okay, we are now ready and willing. Let's now move on to Step Nine.

STEP NINE

Made direct amends to such people wherever possible, except when to do so would injure them or others.

We have made our list and developed an attitude of willingness. So now what? Well, now it's time to make amends. Now we are ready to go out and find those people we have hurt and try to correct our mistakes.

Step Nine is a rebuilding Step. Through it we will be able to rebuild some relationships. Not all relationships, for there may be some people we have hurt who want to have nothing more to do with us.

As we work Step Nine there is a certain attitude we need to have. We must be honest with ourselves. We are doing Step Nine for ourselves because we have harmed these people. Some people may be sad about what we have done to them. Some may be mad at us for the way we have treated them in the past. We must be open to hearing this. If we are not, then we are not yet totally willing to make amends.

We must be ready to listen to the pain and anger of the people we have harmed. If we are still defending ourselves or getting so shameful that we can't hear the other person, we are not ready.

We do not want to come across as A.A. or religious fanatics. We want to be people who have hurt someone else and now want to make things right. We are not hiding behind our illness; we are not afraid to talk about our addiction if asked.

Why are we going to go back? Why can't we let sleeping dogs lie? The answer is that we are trying to rebuild our lives. Our addiction took much, but it took the most from our relationships.

When we used, we acted like no one else in the world mattered. In acting this way we hurt many people. In Step Nine we continue to right the wrongs that our illness caused. We are trying to get back what we have lost. We are working at regaining trust. The loss of trust with family, friends, and others is a major cost of our illness.

We became distrustful people. All alcoholics and other drug addicts, when using, are not trustworthy. Ours is an illness to be mistrusted. We can't be counted on, for we are not in control. Step Nine is about getting honest with this fact to the people who already know it. They know and have known for a lot longer than we have that we were not trustworthy.

We have two ways to build and regain trust:

- *Staying sober.* We become more trustworthy the longer we stay sober. People start to think of us as sober people. The more trust we put in the program, the easier it will be to regain relationships.

- *Working the Ninth Step.* During our using, if we harmed someone, we would deny it. We pretended we were victims of everyone else's behavior. It will be healing for us and others when we go to them and explain exactly how we hurt them, which is what we do in Step Nine.

We feel safer around people who take ownership for their actions. It's easier to forgive people when they are clear with us about how they have behaved badly. This is what Step Nine is about. We are to go and speak with those we have harmed and explain to them exactly what it is that we did that harmed them.

The only time we shouldn't do this is when to do so would injure someone. Step Nine is about healing old wounds, not creating new ones. In this way, it's best to talk over any amends we are going to make with our sponsor and support system.

Let's now look at the different parts of Step Nine.

"Made direct amends to such people wherever possible, . . ."

Step Nine is very clear. We are to go directly to the people we have harmed and make our amends to them personally. We are to do this, "wherever possible." We don't go around them, we go directly to the people we have harmed. We take the list we put together in Step Eight and go talk with these people.

What does it mean to make amends? Let's examine this so it is clear what we are to do.

First and foremost, making amends is not just going to the person and saying, "I'm sorry." These two words get so overused by most addicts that they've come to mean very little. Most of us would say we were sorry a lot and kept right on hurting people. Saying, "I'm sorry" may be a part of Step Nine, but most often it's a very small part.

Making amends means owning up to the fact that we don't play fair with people. They were trying to have a relationship with us and what they really got was a relationship with an addict. We acted as addicts act. We used people. We put people down. We built ourselves up at someone else's expense.

In Step Nine, we go to the people we have harmed and tell them exactly how we have hurt them. Then we ask them what they need from us to set things right. It's not so much saying we're sorry, but saying, "I hurt you, this is how I've hurt you, and what can I do to set things right?"

- If we've stolen money, it's talking with them about how to repay it.
- If we've emotionally damaged someone, now we can help heal the damage.

We'll find most people are very open to talking about amends and are glad to work on finding a way to put the past to rest. There also may be some people who never want to see or speak to us again. If this is the case, then we respect their wishes. Maybe if we stay sober and they have some time to heal, the relationship can be regained, but maybe not.

The reality is that we hurt people, some of them very deeply. The main thing we need to keep in mind is that we are working at becoming responsible people. People who are responsible for *all* their actions.

We will be working Step Nine the rest of our lives. The Step says we should make amends "wherever possible," which means we are open to making amends to anyone we have harmed.

All of us will meet people we've harmed that we didn't think we had harmed. For example, I had an aunt who I only saw every now and then during my using. After I had been sober a couple of years, we met and were talking. She asked me what had changed, so I told her. During our talk, she started crying. I asked her what the tears were about. She talked about seeing me at a family reunion and how worried and upset she was because I looked so sick. She and another aunt were talking and feeling scared for me. Up until then, they weren't on my list, for I didn't think I had caused them pain. I didn't know how many people truly loved me. This is a common mistake for an addict.

". . . except when to do so would injure them or others."

This part of the Step is very clear. We are not to injure anyone as we go about doing our amends. As we meet with people, old hurts and anger may need to be talked through. But we are not to injure anyone. We are not to mess up anyone's life. If bringing up the past will harm their present life and relationships, it's best to work out our amends in another way. The best way to work out these types of amends is through our Higher Power. We can pray that any harm we may have done is taken from the person. This is one clear way we can ask our Higher Power to help us. We may make an agreement with ourselves to say a prayer like this daily for a given period of time.

Perhaps we have stolen money from a former employer and to go back and discuss this would cause undue harm. We can get the money together and send a cashier's check with an anonymous letter about why we are doing this. Or if the business isn't around anymore, we can donate the amount of money to a needy charity.

There is always a way to make amends for past behaviors. If it's not clear to us how, then all we need to do is pray and sometimes, if we listen, we'll get an answer.

Step Nine is a way to right past wrongs.

STEP TEN

Continued to take personal inventory and when we were wrong promptly admitted it.

We have admitted having a very serious illness. We turned over our will and lives to God. We have taken a complete moral inventory of ourselves. We've shared this inventory with another. We've prepared ourselves and asked God to remove our character defects, and we've listed all the people we've harmed and made amends with all of those we could. We've worked hard and changed much.

Step Ten is a safeguard. It keeps us growing in the right direction. We don't want anything to mess up the progress we've made. The best way to be sure of spiritual progress is to make recovery a habit. Step Ten will help us do this. Step Ten is a Step that we should practice each day. This is why it is called a *maintenance Step*. We use Step Ten to look at where we are with our program and to find ways to better it. We want recovery to become second nature to us.

People are always changing. We're either growing into better people or we're sliding back. Step Ten helps us make sure we are moving in the right direction. As we grow older with our sobriety, we will be faced with different tasks. For example, the longer people are in the program, the more likely they are to take the program and Steps for granted. This is normal. The Tenth Step keeps us fresh and alive in our program.

In the Tenth Step inventory, we look for character defects that may be finding their way back into our lives. This is normal. It will happen even if we're working a great program. It is just the way life is. But because of this, we need to take Step Ten very seriously. We check ourselves daily to see if we've been too self-centered. This self-centeredness, or as the Big Book calls it, "self-will," will be at the root of most of the "people problems" we face in recovery. Greed, self-pity, despair, depression, stealing, hatred, controlling behavior, and resentment, all have at their core a strong self-will. So, Step Ten is mainly about keeping a check on our self-centeredness. We are to do this daily. And because we are human, we will not do it perfectly.

There will be times when we are too greedy or too controlling. We are taught in Step Ten what to do then: we *promptly* admit when we are wrong. The Step doesn't say to whom we are to admit our wrongs. Use the Fifth Step for direction on this. When we do find ourselves being wrong, it's best that we admit to God, ourselves, and another human being what we've done wrong. This is a good reason to talk to our sponsor every day. This most likely gets us back on track.

Keeping secrets turns small problems or small character defects into big ones. This is the wisdom behind Step Ten.

- By *promptly* admitting how we're messing up, we don't get into defending our crazy behavior.
- By *promptly* admitting our wrongs, they don't have much of a chance of becoming a solid part of our personality.

We are people who need to be reminded of our defects. By admitting our mistakes and then taking action to correct them, we develop self-respect. We see ourselves as good people who can grow and change and face our problems. Thus, the Tenth Step is a daily boost of self-confidence. If we truly use this Step to maintain our spiritual and emotional growth, self-confidence always follows.

Step Ten is our safety Step. It prevents us from getting too far from our Higher Power, our program, and ourselves. It prevents small problems from becoming big ones. But mainly, Step Ten keeps us connected to ourselves and to our journey of spiritual recovery. If worked daily, Step Ten helps us see when we're starting to get new character defects or when our old ones are popping up again.

Let's now look at the different parts that make up Step Ten.

"Continued to take personal inventory . . ."

As this part of the Step makes clear, taking inventory is not anything new to us. We have done a Fourth Step inventory, and the Eighth Step is an inventory Step also. The fact is that all the Steps have some element of soul-searching in them. Our program leads us into soul-searching. This is how we grow. This is how we're able to achieve *serenity.* Serenity is knowing and accepting who we are and where we fit in.

A member of my A.A. group always talks about how, by continuing to take a personal inventory, he learned two things. First, he learned how to be his own best friend — how to give himself good feedback. Second, he learned how to make The Serenity Prayer part of his life. The Serenity Prayer goes like this:

*God grant me the serenity
To accept the things I cannot change,
The courage to change the things I can,
And the wisdom to know the difference.*

By focusing on a *personal* inventory, my A.A. friend was forced to focus on the true person he could become. He clearly saw the most important words of Step Ten to be "personal inventory." We are not to inventory other people, only ourselves. Also, a personal inventory is one that means something to *us.* We don't just do a surface inventory. We get in there and truly see our behavior and think about why we act in certain ways. The personal inventory will become our main tool to help us with personal growth. It will be our main defense against relapse.

The Little Red Book lists nine key danger signs we're to look for as we do our personal inventory.

1. When we have forgotten that we are alcoholics or other drug addicts — that we have a body that can't handle alcohol and other drugs.
2. When we start taking things for granted and feel grouchy, angry with other people, or expect too much of others.
3. When we ease up on the practice of honesty, humility and making amends.
4. When we become cocky over our A.A. success and stop contact with God.
5. When we lack interest in new members and don't reach out to help them.
6. When we demand power or expect praise for our sobriety.
7. When we get bored.

8. When we start missing A.A. meetings.

9. When we stop studying the A.A. Books.[5]

". . . and when we were wrong promptly admitted it."

This section of the Step is also very clear. When we are wrong, we are to admit it as promptly as we can. Our program is based on honesty. Step Ten puts us to the test. We look at our behavior daily and then try to correct any wrong we find. In this way, we practice being honest people. Self-searching gets easier the more we practice it. And admitting and correcting wrongs gets easier the more we practice it.

Admitting our wrongs also gives us the freedom to move past them once we've done something to correct our behavior. For example, we may find ourselves trying to control someone, and we lose our temper when the person doesn't go along with us. The Tenth Step says that as soon as we realize this wrong, we go back to the person and make amends. By doing this, we allow the wrong of the moment to be a learning point.

Admitting our wrongs to others, especially to those we have wronged, builds trust. Who would you trust? Someone who will admit their mistakes and then try to change for the better, or someone who will not admit to doing anything wrong?

We are all human and make mistakes. This is part of how we learn and grow. By promptly admitting our mistakes, we allow growth to take place. If we don't admit our wrongs, no growth will take place. In fact, the act of not admitting our wrongs is an act of dishonesty.

It is best to admit our wrongs to ourselves, our Higher Power, and someone else — especially to the person involved, if there is one. Sometimes the wrong is against ourselves; then it's still best to tell someone about it.

We learn by talking with others about the ways they've dealt with similar wrongs. By talking with others about our wrongs we get to learn from them. We can use our wrongs for growth instead of hiding them and feeling ashamed. Being wrong is human. Step Ten pushes us to see ourselves and *all* of our humanness.

---

[5] Rephrased from *The Little Red Book.* (Center City, Minn.: Hazelden Educational Materials, 1970), 109-110.

STEP ELEVEN

Sought through prayer and meditation to improve our conscious contact with God as we understood Him, praying only for knowledge of His will for us and the power to carry that out.

Step Eleven is also a maintenance Step. It is about our spiritual maintenance. The Step sets an ongoing goal for us — to improve our conscious contact with our Higher Power. Conscious contact means talking, listening, and feeling. It means we are paying attention to God.

We, as addicts, need this type of goal. Our illness has no cure. We recover by admitting and accepting our illness and then believing in and turning our lives and wills over to our Higher Power. Step Eleven teaches us how to deepen our relationship with our Higher Power.

Why do we keep working at improving this relationship? Isn't just having it enough? The answer is simple: our life depends on this relationship. Remember, we didn't get ourselves sober. Our Higher Power, through these Steps, got us and keeps us sober. Most of us tried to get sober on our own, and it didn't work. Because our program is spiritual, we come to view our daily lives as chances for spiritual growth. Each day gives us opportunities for improvement.

Step Eleven asks us to seek a better relationship with God. Through an ever-improving relationship with our Higher Power, we will learn how to have better relationships with those around us. And the better our relationship is with God, the better our relationship is with ourselves. This is because we see our Higher Power in others. We watch people who were near death, who lost everything, become loving, caring people again. We see their health improve. We see them become responsible citizens again.

In this program, miracles are all around us. We watch our Higher Power in action and we want to become a part of these miracles. We work our program, and we feel and find God inside of us. We feel alive again.

Step Eleven tells us just how we can improve our relationship with our Higher Power through prayer and meditation. The more we pray and meditate, the clearer our relationship with our Higher Power will be.

We can think of prayer as *talking* and of meditation as *listening*. In any relationship, the more we work to improve our communication skills (talking and listening), the better the relationship will be.

Step Eleven speaks about a "conscious contact" with God as we understand Him. What does this mean? It means that we look for and sense God in our everyday life. If we are alert, we'll see our Higher Power all around us — in the seasons, in our sponsors, in the Steps, in our relationships, and in our thoughts and actions.

- Going to check on someone who hasn't been around for a couple of weeks is our Higher Power working through us.
- A small child who says hello to us in a check-out line in the store can remind us of God's presence.

We become aware of the goodness that surrounds us. We become a part of it.

The Step also tells us to pray only for God's will for us and the power to carry that out. We are to work at doing what our Higher Power wants us to do, *not* what we want to do. Maybe we want to correct people's behavior and "set them right," but our Higher Power wants them to learn on their own. We will need some help to resist our will and do what our Higher Power wants. We can pray and ask for this. Step Eleven is like Step Three where we turn our will and lives over to our Higher Power. The Eleventh Step teaches us how to do this better.

Let's look at the parts that make up the Eleventh Step.

"Sought . . ."

The Eleventh Step starts out with the word "sought." This makes it very clear we have a job to do. We are to look for our Higher Power. Step Eleven is an *action Step*. It's a choice — we either do it or we don't. This Step tells us which side to choose. We should remember that a better life doesn't just *happen* — we must do our part.

". . . through prayer and meditation . . ."

Step Eleven tells us how to seek out our Higher Power. We use prayer and meditation. The Step promises this will build a better relationship.

Prayer is simply talking to God, as we understand Him, about what is important in our lives. We give thanks for our new life. We tell our Higher Power of our struggles and also of our successes. We keep the lines of communication open.

Prayer is an *action* on our part. It's an act of surrendering. It's an act of giving our will over to our Higher Power. We can't pray without giving up some part of our own will. As addicts, self-will is very dangerous for us. So we need to pray often.

No one can tell you how to pray. People may guide you, just as this Step does, but remember there is no right or wrong way to pray. Prayer is just talking to your Higher Power. It's not important *how* you do it. Just do it.

Meditation, on the other hand, is listening — listening and slowing ourselves down enough to hear and see our Higher Power around us. Our Higher Power is speaking to us all the time:

- It may be the message we receive at one of our meetings.
- Perhaps it's in the breeze on a warm spring evening.

God is all around us, and meditation is just the act of slowing ourselves down enough to connect with our Higher Power.

Often, our minds are racing so fast we don't hear or see anything around us. We're going too fast. By slowing down and connecting with our Higher Power, we don't have to go it alone. Our Higher Power is with us all the time.

". . . to improve our conscious contact with God
as we understood Him, . . ."

This part of Step Eleven tells us *why* we are to pray and meditate. It is to improve our link with God as we understand Him. The purpose of praying and meditating is just this: to depend on our Higher Power. Why? Because it's our Higher Power who keeps us sober. But this is not all our Higher Power does for us; our Higher Power will help us grow and develop into more loving and caring people. Remember, we've turned our lives and will over to the *care* of our Higher Power.

Our Higher Power is not distant. God is to be close to us and we are to be close to God. We form a deep bond with God. We know where to find God at all times. For many people, God is just an idea. This is not true for us. We have a "conscious contact" with our Higher Power — an ever-present awareness.

**". . . praying only for knowledge of His will for us
and the power to carry that out."**

This part of Step Eleven is like Step Three. In Step Three, we've turned our will and lives over to our Higher Power. Step Eleven tells us how to do that every day. We are to pray to better know God's will for us. This leads us away from self-will and leads us to know God's will.

The key word in this part of the Step is *only*. It makes the Step quite simple. We pray *only* for God's will. This way self-will doesn't get mixed in there. A simple form of this is to pray, "Thy will be done!"

We also pray for the *power* to carry out our Higher Power's will. We will need this power because our Higher Power's will for us is not always easy. We pray for the power to carry out our Higher Power's will. A friend is moving; we have the day free, but we feel lazy. We pray for the power to be helpful.

The Big Book states, "We thought we could find an easier, softer way. But we could not." God's will for us is not always soft or easy. To follow it may take discipline. Discipline is power over ourselves. We are to pray for the power to be spiritual, disciplined people. If we pray for this, our Higher Power will give it to us. It is then up to us to use it.

Step Eleven clearly states that we can have a deep relationship with our Higher Power. It tells us step by step how to get it. Many in the program see this as the most important gift the program has to give.

STEP TWELVE

Having had a spiritual awakening as the result of these steps, we tried to carry this message to alcoholics, and to practice these principles in all our affairs.

Step Twelve is the goal of our journey. It means we are different people. We have been changed as a result of our journey. Step Twelve also tells us where to direct our energy in the future.

Step Twelve speaks about us as different people. We are people who have had a spiritual awakening. Our spirits are alive again. In the past we acted like people who didn't care; now we care deeply. Our illness changed us into people who only cared about ourselves. We came first. We did whatever we wanted when we wanted to do it. We are now people who reach out to others. We have something to give: our story.

The spiritual awakening that this Step speaks about is the best thing the Twelve Steps have done for us. Through the Twelve Steps we have truly become different people.

- We were people who were dying.
- We are now people who are very much alive.
- We were people who took from those around us and gave back very little. We are now people who give to others.

This is truly a miracle. When Step Twelve talks about "spiritual awakening" — it is talking about how *we* are that miracle.

This Step also asks us to serve. We carry the message of our miracles to alcoholics and drug addicts. We are to *try* to help others recover. Why? The main reason is because it will help us stay sober. Remember, all twelve of the Steps help us stay sober.

The founders of this program knew that if we worked at helping others it would do two things:

- It would help keep us busy in a good way and away from bad feelings like self-pity and resentment.
- It would help us feel like good people. It is a way for us to feel good without taking a drug.

It is also a way for us to pay back those who have helped us. We don't pay them back directly. We pay back those who have come before us by helping those who still need help.

This is the Step that teaches us that the Twelve Steps are "principles." Basic truths. It teaches us that the Twelve Steps are basic truths about how to stay sober. We now take these truths we've learned and start to use them in all aspects of our lives. We've learned about acceptance; we've learned about letting go, turning our lives and will over to a loving Higher Power. We've learned how to check ourselves for flaws in how we act. We've learned how to admit when we are wrong. We've learned to pray and we've learned to meditate.

Step Twelve tells us how to take these skills and use them in all parts of our lives. So if we have a problem at work, we think about how our program asks us to handle it. Which principle should we use? The Step is saying, "You now have a conscience; use it in all parts of your life." If we do this, we will stay sober and continue to have spiritual growth. Let's now look at the different parts that make up Step Twelve.

"Having had a spiritual awakening . . ."

Step Twelve says that we have had a spiritual awakening. What a great thing to have happen! It is as if our addiction had put our spirit into a dangerous, dreadful sleep from which it awakens. It's through our spirit that we can feel alive. It's through our spirit that we feel joy. But most importantly, it's through our spirit that we form loving and caring relationships with others. Unless we're aware of our spirit, we can't connect with others. We slowly die of loneliness.

Because of our illness and because of our recovery, we are now different people. We are wiser. We have stopped acting like we can do anything we want, whenever we want. We have stopped saying that what we do doesn't affect anyone but ourselves. We now see how important we are. We see how much we have to give. We see that we need others and they need us.

The spiritual awakening is what we asked for in Step Two. We came to believe we could be restored to sanity. Step Twelve says we have been restored to sanity. It wouldn't ask us to go try and help others if we were still insane!

We admit we are now different and better people. The only question we have to ask ourselves is, *Have I had a spiritual awakening?* Not *Have I had a spiritual experience?* Not *Have I been visited by God?* But *Has my spirit been awakened?* If you feel more alive,

57

if you are acting on your values, and if you are able to stay sober, then it is clear you've had a spiritual awakening.

". . . as the result of these steps, . . ."

Step Twelve asks us to keep in mind how we got our spiritual awakening. We have gotten it through working these Steps. The Steps have made us whole again. Just as our illness showed us how to mess things up, the Steps have shown us how to be spiritual people. This is very important to keep in mind.

The danger is that we can start to think we have done it all by ourselves. If we start to think our own power has restored us to sanity, we are likely to become cocky. This is dangerous for us. We then go it alone and fall back on our addictive ways of behaving. It is very important for us to remember *we have been given sobriety by working these Steps.*

". . . we tried to carry this message to alcoholics, . . ."

This is the part of Step Twelve that most people focus on. It is a statement that we are to *try* to carry the message to others with the same problem. We are only responsible to *try* to carry the message. We are not responsible whether or not the person gets the message; we are just to carry it.

What is the message? The message is that there are Twelve Steps that can keep addicts sober. It is a message of hope. We are to let other addicts, both practicing and recovering, know there is always hope.

How are we to carry this message? The main way we carry this message of hope is just by living our lives, by being loving, sober, and sane people. Many people saw us drunk, high, and insane. Many will also see us become sober.

It's important that *we* realize *we are the message.* We carry the message by staying sober and by living spiritual lives. We are also ready to tell our stories. As the Big Book puts it, we are to tell

- what it was like,
- what happened, and
- what it is like now.

We don't go hanging out in bars and on street corners looking for people to tell our stories to. We have turned this over to our

Higher Power: we are to live the message and our Higher Power will direct us to those we are to help.

- Maybe someone at work or a neighbor will ask us how we were able to change so much. We tell them the truth.
- Maybe friends hint to us that they believe they may have a problem. We let them know we'll be glad to tell them our story. We carry the message by being open.

We also carry the message by going to meetings. The Twelfth Step states we carry the message to alcoholics, as well as to other addicts. This means we also need to help each other. Those of us in recovery need to hear and see others work their program. It keeps us sober.

- We carry the message by getting to our meetings early to make coffee.
- We carry the message by volunteering when there is a task to be done.
- We carry the message by leading the meeting when needed.

". . . and to practice these principles in all our affairs."
The final phrase of the Twelfth Step is "to practice these principles in all our affairs." What are these principles? As stated earlier, they are the basic truths we have learned by working the Steps. These are:

- honesty,
- admitting we're not perfect,
- admitting we need others,
- admitting we need a Power greater than ourselves to run our lives,
- admitting we need to know ourselves, and admitting that all of us have good parts and bad parts.

We know how to be humble and ask for things we need.
We admit we can hurt others, and when we do, we do something about it.
We work at having a better relationship with God, and we learn that prayer and meditation are good for us.
These are some of the principles of the Steps.

Step Twelve tells us to practice the principles, and, like anything else, the more we practice them, the better we know how to use them. We need to practice these principles daily and in every aspect of our lives.

By beginning to practice these principles in all of our affairs, we ask ourselves, *Am I behaving in a way that my Higher Power would want me to?* or *Am I acting in a way I would be willing to share with my group?* We don't act in ways we are ashamed of. We act in ways that help us feel closer to ourselves, our Higher Power, and to others.

We take the program principles with us wherever we go.

- We use them to solve work problems.
- We use them to solve problems in our relationships.
- We use them to tell us how to be friends.
- They will be our guide.

We now have a sense of direction. It may be helpful to think of these principles as the light coming from a lighthouse, warning us of dangers that we cannot see.

Good luck in your spiritual journey and in your sobriety. May your Higher Power watch over you and all of us.